STARTS with You

USA TODAY BESTSELLING AUTHOR
CLAUDIA BURGOA

Also By Claudia Burgoa

Be sure to sign up for my newsletter where you'll receive news about upcoming releases, sneak previous, and also FREE books from other bestselling authors.

Meant For Me

Finally Found You

Where We Belong

Heartwood Lake Secret Billionaires

A Place Like You

Dirty Secret Love

Love Unlike Ours

Through It All

Better than Revenge

Fade into us

An Unlikely Story

Hard to love

Against All Odds Series

Wrong Text, Right Love

Didn't Expect You

Love Like Her

Until Next Time, Love

Something Like Love

Accidentally in Love

Forget About Love

Waiting for Love

Decker Family Novels

Unexpected Everlasting:

Suddenly Broken

Suddenly Us

Somehow Everlasting:

Almost Strangers

Strangers in Love

Perfect Everlasting:

Who We Are

Who We Love

Us After You

Covert Affair Duet:

After The Vows

Love After Us

The Downfall of Us:

The End of Me

When Forever Finds Us

Requiem for Love:

Reminders of Her

The Symphony of Us

Impossibly Possible:

The Lies About Forever

The Truth About Love

Second Chance Sinners :

Pieces of Us

Somehow Finding Us

The Spearman Brothers

Maybe Later

Then He Happened

Once Upon a Holiday

Almost Perfect

Luna Harbor

Finally You

Perfectly You

Always You

Truly You

My One

My One Regret

My One Desire

The Everhart Brothers

Fall for Me

Fight for Me

Perfect for Me

Forever with Me

Mile High Billionaires

Finding My Reason

Something Like Hate

Someday, Somehow

Standalones

Chasing Fireflies

Until I Fall

Christmas in Kentbury

Chaotic Love Duet

Begin with You

Back to You

Co-writing

Holiday with You

Home with You

Here with You

All my books are interconnected standalone, except for the duets, but if you want a reading order, I have it here → Reading Order www.claudiayburgoa.com

Dear Reader,

I write highly emotional romances that include thought provoking subjects. If you would like to see a list of them, please check the link below with more information.

TW Website

Happy Reading,
Claudia

Chapter One

HEARTWOOD LAKE
SECRET BILLIONAIRE SERIES

Callahan

THERE IS a common belief that men and women can't be 'just friends' without any romantic or sexual attraction. Many have tried to prove this theory wrong. There are actual studies that have shown that men and women can indeed have purely platonic relationships.

Do you know what the key to a successful platonic friendship between a man and a woman is?

I have the secret… pretend you don't feel anything for your best female friend.

So far, it's worked for me.

I met Lake Zimmerman in Quantico. She was training to become an agent in the Cyber Crime Division.

There was something about her wit, her brilliance, and her beauty that attracted me to her. We hit it off, but she gently friend-zoned me. In retrospect, that was a wise move on her part. I should've cut my losses then but…

But how can I let her go?

Lake is like a breath of fresh air, and her radiant beauty captivates me instantly.

Her delicate features are like those of a fairy princess, with high cheekbones and soft, kissable lips that seem to be always smiling. Her eyes sparkle with intelligence and wit, a deep shade of green that seems to see straight into my soul.

She moves with an almost otherworldly grace. She's barely five foot four. No one would ever guess she's a lethal FBI agent who could easily take a six-foot-four man down with just a few moves.

Lake is not only a valuable asset as a work colleague, but she's also my best friend… and dare I say that she's the love of my life. I've never admitted to anyone—let alone myself—my deep-seated love for her that threatens to consume me every day. The thought of losing her, of never seeing her again, sends a shiver down my spine.

I can't bear the thought of living without her, and yet, here we are in the midst of something that could very well end up costing not only my life but more importantly hers. But somehow we've found ourselves knee-deep in the nine circles of hell.

How did I let this happen?

What if there's no escape?

I wish I could claim her being here was a simple accident. I would use any excuse I could to be in her presence, work related or not. I invited her to my house so I could utilize her forte of piecing things together with ease while we discussed the case Ryder and I got assigned two weeks ago. I figured with her particular skill set, she could help us considering this was a case I couldn't exactly back away from, since it involves my father and the DiGiacomo Family.

Was I surprised to discover my father was married into the Italian mafia?

Nothing that involves him surprises me.

Nothing.

Until this, I wasn't expecting the unfortunate events that followed. First, my father was found dead in his office. Second, an intruder broke into my house, attempting to kill me. Third, the family vacation home in Vermont was set on fire.

There's no doubt that someone is after us.

We escaped unscathed. Ansel, my best friend, was able to call in a few favors to evacuate my family, and now...

well, I'm in a sketchy hotel hiding out until he can tell me where we go next.

"Are you sure you're okay?" I ask again as Lake takes off her bloody jacket and tosses it onto the floor.

She hasn't uttered a word since we left my house, not one peep. I've barely received a brief glance. Her green eyes seem lost, but I know better. She's working something out and is not ready to tell me what it is. The weight of the unspoken words between us hangs heavy in the air, suffocating me with uncertainty and fear.

"Lake." I press my lips together. "Talk to me, darling. You're scaring me."

She touches the side of her neck and sighs. "I'm okay."

Is she? Because that asshole had a knife against her and I'm still trembling with fear. I almost lost her—and I don't even have her. I wish I could hold her close to allay my fears and whisper that everything will be okay. But what happens if I cross the line and fuck up our friendship?

"You didn't allow me to fight him," she snarls as she heads toward the bathroom. "We could've interrogated him. Instead, you shot him."

She turns on the shower. "And to make matters worse, you made me leave my phone behind."

"We deleted everything. It's safe."

As Lake gazes at me, her expression seems to convey a sense of pity, as if to say, "You poor clueless man."

And I obviously don't understand why she's so upset about losing her phone. Before I can ask, she begins to shrug out of her clothes. She takes off the hair tie she wears, allowing her luscious dark curls to cascade down her shoulders. However, some locks are caked with dried blood.

"I'm guessing your dad was seriously involved with *them*," she whispers the last word.

"Sorry, I didn't mean to drag you into this with me."

Her eyes pierce through me with an intense glare, and with one forceful push, the tattered remains of her clothing fall to the ground. Standing before me, she appears stunningly bare, an image I never thought I'd ever have the chance to witness.

I never entertained the fantasy where we became more than friends, let alone shared a bath. Suppressing my feelings for so long has become unbearable, and now they're bubbling up inside me, threatening to overflow at any moment. As I gaze at her in this vulnerable state, I realize how much I love her, how my heart aches with longing to hold her close and confess everything I've denied myself.

But I keep my mouth shut. This isn't the place or the moment. I have to figure out how to keep us safe while finding out who killed my father.

"Can we discuss what happened?" I insist.

Without hesitation or another word, Lake strides into the shower, shutting her eyes as the water cascades down her body, tracing every soft curve and contour until it meets the drain. She stands beneath the warm stream, washing away the horrors of what almost happened to us.

The water runs red with the blood that has stained her

hair and skin, a stark reminder of the scariest moment of my life. My heart aches with the intensity of my emotions, feeling every bit of her pain as if it were my own. As the water continues to flow, I am struck by the depth of my feelings for her, and this fierce desire to protect her at any cost.

"You didn't trust me," she says, her eyes remaining closed.

"I couldn't just let him…" I pause, not knowing how to finish the sentence. I've guarded my secret for years, and I should continue doing so, but I almost lost her. "I can't lose you, Lake."

She moves slightly away from the cascading water, runs a hand down her face, and finally opens her eyes.

"Lose me?" She furrows her brow in frustration, her eyes narrowing as she stares at me. "Do you not have any faith in my abilities? I am a trained agent, capable of defending myself in any situation. You didn't trust me to be capable." Her words reverberate throughout the bathroom, echoing off the walls with a fierce intensity that leaves no doubt as to the strength of her conviction. Her anger simmers just beneath the surface. I feel as if I failed her in some way or another.

"I just wanted to make sure you were safe," I reply, my voice strained with emotion. I take a deep breath, trying to calm the rising tension between us. "In that moment, you weren't Agent Zimmerman. You were Lake. *My Lake.* The love of my life."

She gawks at me. "Excuse me?"

I clear my throat. "I know. This isn't the time or the place to tell you that I'm madly in love with you and that those seconds took years away from me. I feared I would lose you—and I couldn't let him take you away from me."

Her gaze softens. "Cal..."

I join her in the shower. The hot steam swirls around us, and the sound of the water cascading down our bodies in a steady rhythm that's almost hypnotic. I step in front of her, and take her in my arms, feeling the warmth of her body.

"We..." she trails her voice but not her gaze. We look into each other's eyes, and I see it, the fear that she had hidden all too well until now.

I caress her wet hair, and she laughs, though the humor doesn't reach her eyes. "Aren't you going to undress?"

I smirk. "Is that an invitation?"

"Make me forget," she says. "Can you... I need a moment to stop the madness inside my head. Could you do this for me?"

I quickly undress and toss my soaking clothes outside the shower before pulling her deeper into my embrace. Lake's lips part in an invitation, and I eagerly accept. The moment our mouths touch, we ignite with a passionate hunger that consumes us.

I'm lost in the moment.

Our kiss deepens, exploring each other fervently with a desperation that races shivers up my spine. Every nerve in my body is electrified as I savor this searing kiss, that I never want to end. Our bodies move together in perfect harmony.

The heat and the steam and her body all conspire to send me spinning into a state of passion. I move my hands over her curves, her skin like silk beneath my fingertips. I want to touch her everywhere, feel her softness against mine.

As we explore each other's bodies, I try to push away the thoughts of everything that happened and focus on this moment, but it's almost impossible.

"Cal," Lake stops me in my tracks. "Stay with me. You're supposed to make me forget, not remind me of what we went through tonight."

She's right. She's finally here, with me. We're together, but this isn't the way I want it to happen. I want our first time to be unforgettable.

Chapter Two

Lake

AM I MAKING A MISTAKE?

On the one hand, I always wanted to know how Callahan Thorndale tastes. And I've discovered he tastes like nothing I've ever experienced before—a delicious blend of sweet and earthy, with a hint of something dark and mysterious.

Do I want to continue kissing him?

Probably. I can't get enough of him. It's hard to stop myself from exploring the contours of his mouth with my own, savoring every moment of this intoxicating kiss. I need more of him with a fierceness that scares me and yet feels right.

His kiss.

It's like a bolt of lightning striking right through me, igniting every nerve and setting me ablaze. It makes me feel truly alive—consumed by passion and desire.

But this isn't me. I'm usually all about being cool and collected, but this one kiss from Callahan Thorndale has me feeling like a completely different person.

I mean, just feeling my lips still tingling from the electricity of that initial kiss, I can't help but wonder... am I falling for him? It's like he's this irresistible force that just tears down all my carefully constructed walls and settles himself right in the center of my being.

Am I in love with him?

I try not to think about feelings, not when I have to focus on my job... and I have two of them.

Do I find him attractive?

Callahan has a handsome face. Chiseled jawline and sharp cheekbones that could make any woman weak in the knees. And don't even get me started on that rugged, alluring look he's got going on—it's like he's straight out of a romance novel. A novel where the lead male character is Henry Cavill or Chris Pine.

But it's not just his physical appearance that's got me all hot and bothered (though, let's be real, that hair is begging to be touched). No, it's those piercing blue eyes that seem to bore straight into my soul, conveying both authority and tenderness in one fell swoop. And when he flashes that killer smile, I swear every woman within a ten-mile radius starts shedding their clothes—not necessarily me.

But here's the thing: I'm not just any woman.

Sure, he's got a tall, broad-shouldered frame that he carries with the confidence of a man who knows he could have anyone he wants. But he can't have me. I don't care about some guy who thinks he's God's gift to women.

Nope.

I do like the hint of vulnerability in his demeanor. That makes me want to wrap my arms around him and ask him to kiss me again until I can't breathe—or think about anything but him.

Move away from his embrace, I tell myself as he finishes washing the blood away from me. He lathers my body with soap but doesn't touch me in those aching places begging for his long fingers.

Move.

Lake Sophia Hawkins Zimmerman, move now.

But of course, I don't move. Instead, I allow him to finish washing me.

He reaches out for a towel. Every fiber of my being is screaming at me to move, run, and stop letting this happen. Do anything but allow him to touch me, because if I do, I might do something very, very stupid. Like surrender my heart and falling madly in love. But I can't resist him. I need this.

I need him.

I stay still, allowing him to wrap the scratchy fabric around my shoulders and begin to gently dry me off. His touch is tender, and as he works his way down my body, I can't fight the awakening within me—the flicker of desire.

It's a spark of something that I have buried deep within myself for far too long.

As he finishes drying me off, he reaches for my hand and leads me to the bed. I am still naked, vulnerable, and completely at his mercy. But even as the fear and anger rage inside me, I can't help but feel a strange sense of peace. In this moment, all that matters is the touch of his skin against mine, the warmth of his body next to me, and the way his breath tickles my neck.

Cal leans in close and whispers, "Lake." The way he says my name hits me right at the center of my heart, and I'm lost.

Lost in the moment.

Lost in his touch.

Lost in the overwhelming emotions that threaten to consume me.

I feel my self-control slipping away, giving it to Callahan. I no longer care if this is a mistake I'll regret. This moment, as his lips brush against mine, I don't care. I need this.

I need to lose myself to something other than the fear

and emptiness that I have been feeling since I had that knife held to my throat.

"Lake, baby, are you sure about this?" His voice is soft and hesitant.

"Yes." My voice is barely audible. "I'm sure."

As I speak those words, my heart feels like it's about to burst out of my chest, racing with a wild, almost uncontrollable intensity. I'm overwhelmed with a rush of desire, and I can't help but feel like I'm teetering on the edge of a cliff.

I'm teetering on the brink of madness.

I'm teetering on a narrow beam above an ocean of emotions.

It's like I'm standing on a tightrope, with one wrong move threatening to send me tumbling to the void.

Cal's mouth hovers over mine, lingering a moment before he kisses me. His hands caress a path up my leg all the way to my torso. I open my legs, pushing my hips up, wanting some relief. He releases my mouth and his lips curve slightly, as he nuzzles my neck, whispering, "I'm in charge, Lake."

The way he says my name as if it's an order but also a prayer makes me shiver, and I tremble when his fingers tease my nipple. I clench my legs, arching my hips again but he doesn't even acknowledge my need. He just teases my breasts with his mouth. Suckling. Nibbling.

"Don't play with me," I pant out.

The satisfaction in his deep blue eyes is almost as big as his desire. He presses his lips to my sternum and begins to feather kisses down to my lower body. Simultaneously, his fingers find my wet heat. I release a throaty moan as he finally begins to ease the ache that's about to overwhelm me.

He drags one of my legs to his shoulder before his mouth lowers and finds my clit. Fingers, mouth, and tongue lapping, nibbling, kissing, thrusting. My heart pounds in my chest, racing faster and faster as the pleasure builds and builds.

I'm lost in a haze of pure sensation, every inch of my skin tingling as I reach the peak of pleasure, the tension coiling tighter and tighter inside me until it's almost unbearable. And then, with a loud cry of his name on my lips, I shatter into a million pieces, my body convulsing with the force of my release.

There's no time for me to react. He's already on top of me, his mouth closes down on mine, and I taste myself on his lips. I'm desperate for more, for him, for his body. There's no slow burn, only a fire with flames so high I can't see anything but the inferno around me.

His thick erection teases my hip. I'm about to reach for it when he says, "I need to be inside you."

Please is all I say, and he presses his length inside me. I pant with the sensation of him sliding deep. Deeper. So deep. It takes me some time to get used to him. When he begins to thrust in and out, he takes my mouth.

As he kisses me, I want more. I want him to take all of

me. I want him to possess me slowly or quickly, but either way, make me all his.

I want him to slowly reveal every layer of my being until there is nothing left but his mark upon me. I crave to feel the intensity of his passion, to be consumed by his desire. To burn me with his flames and take my soul, but to give me his heart.

While he pushes himself in and out and I meet his thrusts, all I want is to let go. I am willing to give myself to him completely.

To surrender to him, body and soul, to be his forevermore.

And as he holds me close, I feel a sense of belonging, a sense of home that I have never felt before. This shouldn't be happening. He's my best friend and I don't have time to... but all I want is this. Us.

I can't think more as the waves of pleasure wash over me. I feel him shudder and groan, his own release finally breaking free. We collapse onto the bed, our bodies entwined and spent, and I know this moment has changed us forever.

"I love you," he says and as much as I want to say the same, something stops me from doing so. Callahan Thorndale is important to me, but we can't be. Not when he doesn't know who I really am.

Chapter Three

HEARTWOOD LAKE
SECRET BILLIONAIRES SERIES

Callahan

ANSEL ARRIVES PRECISELY when he said he would. He drives us in a dark sedan to an undisclosed off-the-grid remote location. The only thing that breaks the eerie silence is the sound of tires on the loose gravel. I can feel Lake's unease. Her eyes are heavy and uneasy as we leave civilization behind us.

We arrive at an airstrip I've never been to before. A private jet stands tall, glimmering in the moonlight. Ansel guides us on board and excuses himself to a back room with no explanation. As the engines roar to life I'm overcome with a sense of dread, but soon we are gliding through clouds, flying further away from home.

When we land, we're not at a hangar or an international airport. Instead, we find ourselves on a remote landing strip nestled between evergreens.

"Where are we?" I ask at the same time Lake says with urgency, "I need to go home."

"Welcome to Heartwood Lake, Colorado," Ansel says.

I try not to glare at him or snap, but I can't help myself. "Where the fuck did you take us?"

Lake looks around and shakes her head. "I need to go home," she insists.

"Don't get snippy with me," Ansel warns me. "I did what you requested. I saved your ass and made sure no one found out. Do you think it was easy to convince my bosses to get you into this program?"

I blink a couple of times. "What program?"

"Endor Concealment," Ansel responds. "This is a private WITSEC run by Crait Quantum Shield, a high intelligence security company, and the sheriff of this town."

"I don't need to be in WITSEC," I argue.

He pats my shoulder. "Oh, but you do." He tilts his head. "Follow me. The Boss wants to discuss the next steps with you."

I grab Lake's hand and we make our way to a golf cart. Under different circumstances, I would joke about the setting. Is this a prank? Ansel used to be part of the FBI and my partner, and in our spare time, we used to play practical jokes on each other. However, Ans left the FBI a few years ago and now works for a private company. I assume it's Crait Quantum Shield—I've never heard of them before.

Lake groans. "I need a phone."

Ansel shakes his head and gives me an exasperated look. "You waited so many years, and now…"

"Leave it," I say.

"I'm not sure what you two are talking about, but I need to go home—or at least get to a phone," she insists.

"Once you're here, you can't leave or contact anyone," Ansel warns her.

"We'll figure this out," I say to Lake reassuringly, but her eyes flicker with anger and annoyance. Doesn't she get that we were almost killed, and that her life is in danger?

Speaking of danger, I remember that I'm not the only Thorndale who should be under Ansel's protection. "Where's my family?"

"They're already in their cabins resting," Ansel responds. "Lake, does anyone know you're with Callahan?"

She shakes her head, but she's looking at the trees. There's no way for me to know if she's lying or not.

"Maybe we can send you home—if no one can trace you to the Thorndale family."

Lake snorts. "I know how to keep myself invisible. Just let me go back home," she insists.

WE ARRIVE AT A CONFERENCE ROOM, and my gaze is immediately drawn to the two imposing figures standing in front of the giant screens on the wall.

"Boss, he's here," Ansel announces.

The older man turns around and I pause for a beat. He towers above my six three, his piercing dark eyes scanning me from head to toe. His furrowed brow might indicate he's all business. The second man, who is younger and just as tall, finally turns to look at us. His silver eyes narrow as they study Lake and then me.

"I don't think we need to be in WITSEC, sir, but I appreciate your help," I say to no one in particular. My voice exudes confidence and authority.

But deep down, I'm terrified. The thought of having to uproot my life, leave everything behind, and go into hiding is overwhelming. I never imagined I'd find myself in this situation.

"You need it," he says, his eyes piercing mine. "My gut says you're underestimating the DiGiacomo Family. There's a rumor they have informants from organizations—including the FBI. If you go back..." He waves his hand dismissively. "You won't survive more than a day."

My mind races as I try to process his words. Is it really

that bad? Could they really have that much power and reach? I feel a knot form in my stomach as I consider the consequences of ignoring his warning. My father is dead, and I almost lost Lake…

I take a deep breath, trying to calm myself down. Maybe he's right. Perhaps I don't need the protection, but my family does. I might not like some of them, but I can't in good conscience let them die.

"Hi, Archer." Lake takes a step forward. "I don't have anything to do with this. I would like to head home if you don't mind."

I can feel the tension in the air, and I know something is off. The younger man's jaw twitches, and I can sense his anger simmering just below the surface. "The name is Finnegan Gil," he says, his voice laced with irritation. "You're confusing me with someone else."

Lake smiles as if trying to diffuse the situation. "Probably. I apologize. You look a lot like a family friend—my father and uncles mentored him when he was young."

I'm confused by her words, and my mind struggles to make sense of it all. "Your father, the tattoo artist?" I ask, my eyebrows furrowing in confusion. How does a tattoo artist have any connection to a man who works for a security company? Did Lake hit her head?

Finnegan smiles. "It happens more often than you can imagine." He tilts his head toward the man next to him. "Derek can show you the town, Miss…"

"Lake Zimmerman. I'm an FBI agent, but I was born in

Seattle," she responds, and I don't understand why she's giving him so many details about her life.

"D, would you mind taking care of our guest while I discuss with Mr. Thorndale why he has to stay with us."

"She should stay," I say. "She mentioned that she's also FBI and could help us with whatever you need to know."

Finnegan shakes his head. "If we need her later, we'll call her."

Lake doesn't protest. She leaves without giving me a second glance. What am I missing?

Chapter Four

Lake

Everything has gone to shit.

Everything.

Things Lake screwed up before the week is over:

I almost got killed.

I slept with my best friend.

Somehow I landed myself in WITSEC, and I don't

know how to get out of this one without blowing my cover.

Fuck.

All the people who were counting on me are going to be pissed. What can I say? Umm, I'm sorry, but I'm stuck here. The weight of the situation is crushing me, and I feel like I'm suffocating. My mind is racing a mile a minute, and I'm just hoping and praying that this man can help me.

I start with a simple question, "So, he still doesn't remember he's Archer, huh?"

Derek glances at me and doesn't say a word.

"Listen, I just need to go home."

"Let's get to the house, and we can discuss your situation," he says without batting an eyelash or smiling at me.

Somehow, he reminds me of my father. He takes his role too seriously while working. He's so stoic, that it's almost unnerving. It's like he's a robot, programmed to do his job and nothing more. I can't help but wonder if he's a former special op. There's something about his demeanor that screams Navy Seal, Delta Force, or a Ranger.

I just need to find the tattoos that will give him away, or… "My father is—"

"I need you to stop talking," he growls as we make our way cautiously through the eerie town of Heartwood Lake.

This is the first I have heard of this place. I scan my surroundings with intrigue and awe. The buildings are aging, their walls crumbling and stained with age, but still with an enchanting charm that's hard to resist.

Walking down the streets, I'm entranced by the beauty

around me. The snowcapped peaks rise in the distance like monsters, their tops gleaming in the sunlight. The crisp air fills my lungs with warmth yet dread.

Despite its size, there are plenty of businesses: a general store, a hardware store, a café next to an ice cream parlor, and even a tiny bookstore. But the locals need to be more friendly. They just throw me glances and nod as I pass by.

"Lake!" My name rings across the street, and I spot Donna Foster, Callahan's mom, amidst her two sons—Magnus and Bach.

I wonder if the rest of the Thorndale siblings are here. Cal has eight of those, if I don't count the baby born last month. His mother is trying to prove he's the legitimate son of Eric Thorndale. For the sake of the baby's future, let's hope he isn't related.

"Hi, Ms. Foster," I greet her, and she takes me in her arms.

"So glad to see you," I say, disentangling myself from her embrace.

"I wish I could say the same but…" She glances around and leans closer to me. "Do you know what's happening? They don't want to tell us anything." Her smile fades away as she touches her lips and then lowers her hand back by her side.

"Mom," Magnus whispers urgently. "Remember they said not to speak freely here."

She touches her lips with the tip of her fingers. "It's like we're in prison—is this safe?"

"It is," I assure her, then add, "Are all your siblings in town?"

Magnus shrugs. "Not only them, but a few others also made it too."

Bach rolls his eyes but doesn't say a word.

"We have to go," Derek says. He focuses on Donna, Magnus, and Bach. "We'll see you later today, as planned."

Donna throws me a glance. One full of sorrow then she quickly turns away from me before I can see any emotion further in her eyes.

As soon as I enter the cabin, Cal's voice echoes through the room, and his face contorts into a frown. "Where have you been?" His voice is demanding. Knowing him, he's been worried sick about my whereabouts. The tension building in the air is almost suffocating.

I take a deep breath, trying to steady my nerves. "No need to worry," I reply, my voice calm and measured. "I was just going through orientation and getting to know this lovely town. Do you know they don't have computers in the library?"

He's not a technology geek like me, but I expect him to crack some joke. He doesn't. He looks me up and down, his eyes lingering on my outfit. "Those aren't the clothes Ansel gave you," he observes.

I could say something like, 'no kidding, Sherlock,' or

'what gave it away?' But this isn't the time to let my smart-mouth loose.

Still, I sass him while smoothing my leggings and fixing the long sweatshirt I got while visiting Derek and his wife. "Well, this fits a lot better than his clothes, don't you think? You can even see my boobs."

Cal's expression softens slightly, but I can still sense his apprehension. "Good, I'm glad you're getting comfortable," he says, his voice low and serious. "I just learned that we're not going home anytime soon."

I can feel a lump forming in my throat. I hate to keep things from him, but for his sake and mine I have to do it. After midnight, I'll be on my way to Seattle and afterward, I should be back in DC. No one will notice I was missing or know that I was with Cal.

So, I play dumb. "How so?"

"It's complicated, and unfortunately, I'm not authorized to disclose anything to anyone—not even you or my family," he mumbles, as if trying to make sure no one is listening. "I'm sorry for dragging you into this with me."

"I deserve a little more than the crappy orientation, the clothes, and your pity, don't you think?" I straighten my shoulders, feigning hurt.

"This is just…" The sound of a phone interrupts him. I frown when I see him pull it out of his pocket.

"You brought yours, but I had to leave mine?" I snap at him.

"They gave it to me. It's…" He runs a hand through his hair. "Listen, it's Ryder. I need to take this call."

Chapter Five

HEARTWOOD LAKE
SECRET BILLIONAIRES SERIES

Callahan

I ANSWER the phone once I'm outside the cabin. "Thorndale speaking."

"Where are you?" Ryder mumbles.

"It's not important," I manage to say, my voice barely above a whisper.

Ryder's scoffing tone cuts through my inner turmoil. "What do you mean it's not important? Your father is dead, Thorndale. And they think you're involved."

"That's the thing. I don't know shit," I lie. "I was hoping you would fill in the blanks. Why did someone try to attack me in my own apartment?"

"What?" There's shock in his voice. Finnegan Gil might be wrong, and he's on my side. Still, I can't tell him where I am or what's happening.

"Sorry, but I don't have anything," he says. "All I know is that they're looking into everyone close to you and... they can't find your family."

"What do you mean?" I try my best to sound worried, but not concerned enough that he'll be suspicious. After all, he knows I don't give two fucks about most of my family.

"Magnus hasn't been at the office all week," he mentions my eldest brother. "Bach's last whereabouts was the teacher's lounge at Columbia."

"Mag is probably fucking some blonde," I respond since we both know my brother is a manwhore. "He is always off on some sexual escapade."

"What about your sisters?"

I scoff. "I already told you to stay away from them. Gen and Elle are off-limits," I say with a warning tone. "They don't need someone like you."

He chuckles. "That's not what I mean, Thorndale," he says with amusement evident in his tone. "I just wanted to know if you knew where they're at, but then again I should know better than to ask you since you're a shitty brother."

He's wrong. I'm a great brother to Magnus and Bach. Mom taught us to be supportive of each other. The rest of my siblings are… an inconvenience at best. I wouldn't care who Elmira or Genevieve date, but I definitely need to make sure they're not close to men like Ryder.

And though I can barely stand six of my eight siblings, I made sure Ansel got them here and away from the mess my father left behind.

"How about—"

"Before you continue naming all of them," I interrupt him, my voice laced with frustration and impatience. "I'll stop you right there and remind you that I don't give a fuck about any of them. Therefore, I have no idea where Gael, Gen, Slade, Drake, River, or Elle are."

"Well, just letting you know we can't find any of them," he informs me, his tone heavy with worry and apprehension.

"What are you implying? Are you telling me they might be dead or in danger?" I pretend to be in shock, masking my true emotions.

"Sorry, man," he says, his voice filled with regret and sympathy. "Do you know who else is missing?"

"Is that a rhetorical question, or do you want me to start guessing?" I snap at him, clearly annoyed. "This isn't the time to play the guessing game. You're telling me that my family is in danger—and we know I was almost killed last night."

"Lake Zimmerman went missing last night," he says with a tone that sounds like, 'take that, Callahan Thorndale. She's gone.'

"What? What do you mean missing?" I demand, pretending to be anxious and fearful of her whereabouts.

"No one can find her," he says. "I was wondering if you know where she could be since you two are... close."

I try to keep my cool. "What do you mean by that?"

"Nothing. I'm just telling you what I know and wondering if you have any information," he explains.

"I haven't seen her," I lie through my teeth, hoping that this doesn't cost her her job or, worse, her life.

Nothing will happen to Lake. She's staying with me until we get to the bottom of this clusterfuck.

"What if she's a mole working for the DiGiacomo Family?" he suggests, and I feel a surge of disbelief and betrayal.

"Are you serious?" I snap, my voice rising with anger. "You think Lake could be the one responsible for all this? That's absurd."

"She's always hiding her whereabouts. No one knows much about her family. Her file is too clean," he argues.

I feel a lump form in my throat. Just earlier today she released some information I'd never heard before. She's from Seattle. We're best friends. I should know more about her.

"Do you know that she was born and raised in Alabama?" he adds.

The last question is a punch in the gut. I could assume he's fishing for information, but after hearing, she's not from DC as I assumed, I'm starting to wonder if Lake is hiding anything more from me.

What if she is?

There has to be a perfect explanation as to why I don't know some important facts about her. I know the basics. She's a twin. Her father is a tattoo artist, and her mother is a doctor. She has two younger brothers. They're close, but she avoids seeing her family because work is more important. I sigh and wonder if Ryder is trying to throw me with useless facts to see if I'll slip and tell him whatever I know.

"I'll be gone for a while," I say.

"I'm sure we can prove that you didn't kill your father. Come back," he says.

It's not dear old dad who concerns me, but the mess he left behind.

"Give me a few days, okay?"

"Fine, I'll call you at this number soon," he says before hanging up.

I hope this conversation was long enough so Finnegan and his people can work their hacking magic—whatever that entails. They're hoping Ryder will continue to be in charge of the case or at least be part of the investigation.

Is this a good idea?

Staying in this small town, working with their company

while we figure out how to take down the DiGiacomo Family. But also searching for the person who killed my father and continuing to protect my family. I might not care about them in the conventional way, but they're Thorndales and it's my duty to keep them safe.

Do I have any other choice?

Chapter Six

Callahan

I STEP INTO THE HOUSE, and Lake is already pacing the living room, her brow furrowed. When she notices me, her face shifts to apprehension, and she asks with an edge to her voice, "Everything okay?"

I nod in response.

She plants her hands on her hips, her eyes narrowing as she says, "So you have a phone."

"Only temporary," I counter vaguely. "I'm not sure what they want to do with the information I can gather from a few calls I made to some key players."

Lake nods, studying me, and I know she's trying to figure out what happened during the call. She's curious and more so when it's something that affects her. I don't want to bring up my discussion with Finnegan, so I decide to move on to the next tricky subject—us. "So, we're going to be stuck in this town for the unforeseeable future. And I was thinking… that maybe you and I could try dating."

Her lips press together in thought before she points out with unwavering focus she repeats, "We're in the middle of a crisis."

"If you went through orientation," I remind her, looking up to catch her gaze, "then they told you that you have to try living as normal a life as possible during our time here."

"They're looking into taking me out of the program," she suddenly drops a bombshell.

My heart sinks. Stunned, my jaw slackens, and I ask incredulously. "No, why? You almost got killed."

With a defensive posture, Lake responds defiantly, "But I didn't."

A swell of emotion rises within me at the memory of how close she had come to losing her life. "Lake, don't you see it? I need you close so I can protect you. We…" I trail off, my voice and gaze faltering.

But I don't continue because what if Lake isn't who I think she is? Is she a mole?

Fuck.

That call with Ryder messed me up. Why did I let him get into my head? Lake isn't like that. She would never betray me.

I clear my throat, pushing back the doubt, and suggest quickly, trying to change direction. "We could work at the bar. I heard they have two openings there."

She snorts while rolling her eyes, her mouth turning down in a frown. "What are you talking about?"

Lifting my gaze to meet hers again, I slowly explain, "As I mentioned, we're staying here for a while. During our time here, we need to become productive members of society. That includes getting jobs, and helping out with the ranch."

Lake cocks her head slightly and gives me a skeptical look. "Why are we helping with the ranch?"

"It's necessary," I state firmly. "We moved here to help Uncle…" I snap my fingers, trying to remember the name of the town's sheriff.

She laughs, obviously amused by my ineptitude. "You need a lot of training before you can go outside and mingle with the townies. You don't even like people."

Folding my arms across my chest defensively, I question her knowledge. "You act as if you know what you're doing here? You think you'll become little miss congeniality?"

Her expression sobers, and her lips form a tight line. "For your information, I'm here by mistake, but if I had to stay, I would blend in flawlessly."

Regret fills me, and I feel guilty for dragging her into this mess. Apologetically, I admit, "I'm sorry." My voice is a remorseful whisper lingering into the still air.

"We didn't know this would happen," she replies softly, though her eyes remain intense on mine. She releases a heavy breath before adding quietly, "So what now?"

"Since we can adopt a new personality and life, why don't we say you're my fiancée, and we live together?" I suggest, my heart pounding in my chest.

My proposal is met with an exasperated groan. "Cal…" she starts but trails off without saying more.

"When I said that I love you, I meant it. I do. And not just like a friend. I want you. The beautiful, brilliant, sassy woman who doesn't take shit from anyone. I admire your strength and—"

"Cal, you're a catch, but we can't start a relationship in the middle of a crisis," she repeats. "That's a terrible foundation. Plus, I'm going—"

"You can't go home," I insist firmly.

She stands defiantly and gives me a glare. "We have to stop interrupting each other. In this case, neither one of us is wrong or right. You have your family to consider—all of them are in town. All. Of. Them."

A groan escapes my lips as the reality of the situation hits me in full force. She might be right. Mom, Flora—Dad's wife number two—are here. My father's children and… this will be a circus.

"Don't stress out," she claims soothingly, stepping closer and cupping my cheeks tenderly in her delicate hands. "Under different circumstances, I'm sure we could have had an amazing relationship. One for the books."

"You think so?" I ask, not arguing with her because she might claim that this won't work out, but I have plenty of time to prove her wrong. Maybe even years.

She nods with sincerity and vulnerability swimming in her eyes.

"Are you telling me that you like me? Or maybe you love me?" I whisper hesitantly, barely daring to breathe.

In response, she rises onto her tiptoes and places a featherlight kiss upon my lips, sending sparks shooting through my body. Desperate to prolong the moment, I tighten my grip around her waist and deepen the kiss hungrily. Every cell in my body hums with electricity.

"Cal," she whispers my name with a raspy voice filled with lust.

Something changes in the air. There's a radical shift, and I feel it, echoing inside me. It's not her words, not her voice; it's the hunger in her dark green eyes.

My lips caress her skin. I'm not hesitant, just cautious. I want this to be different from last night. I was gentle but desperate to feel alive, to meld our souls and make her mine. Today... today, I want to convince her that we don't need to wait for another life. I want her to know we can be good together, even when things are fucked up.

All I want is to kiss her forever, to make love to her forever. Show her that we're two parts of a whole that shouldn't be apart.

That we belong together.

She's the woman I've been waiting for my entire life. Now that I have her I don't want to let her go. We're destined. But I don't think words can convey everything she needs to know to accept us.

This, my surrender has to be it.

Just kissing her isn't enough.

Lake's hands curl around my neck. She's kissing me with the same hunger I carry, and she's as worked up as I am.

She moans and groans as my hands fidget with her clothes. I can't stop myself, and I hope she lets me continue.

Lake's trembling hand stroke over the hard ridge in my pants. I don't expect her to pull the zipper and release my hard as fuck length, but that's exactly what she does. Her palm grabs my heavy cock, and she rubs it, tugging at it.

Fighting my desire, I grasp the single drop of self-control I have left to slow things down and stop kissing her. She's lost in a trance, but I don't want to rush this time, so I find a way to bring her back. My heart kicks into a fast-pounding tempo as I stare into her lustful eyes.

The heat between us surges, once again, as she pulls me down to her, deepening the kiss, drawing me closer, and making me forget that we're in the middle of a fucked up situation in a town that might not be found on a map.

I move my lips toward her jaw and then her neck.

"Don't make me wait," she mumbles. "Don't tease me. I want you inside. Now."

My body trembles with pleasure as I kiss her neck, pushing her further against the couch. The force of our union rumbles through her like a thunderstorm. We move together in synchronized harmony, letting out moans of hunger and love.

She wraps her legs around me, kissing my shoulder with every thrust.

Our passion reaches heights unknown, as we become one and our souls fuse. As our souls merge, I am overcome with a sense of euphoria. A feeling of oneness that is both exhilarating and terrifying. Nothing else matters except the overwhelming moment we're sharing—the love.

But will she ever love me?

I don't have any more time to dwell on that thought, as I feel it like current running throughout my body, giving me the strength to plunge into her harder and faster.

With each deep thrust, I can feel the pulse of our energy creating waves upon waves that we're harnessing into an all-consuming power. As our hearts beat faster in tandem, we reach the peak of ecstasy, the pressure at the base of my spine forcing us both to break into a million pieces.

As our bodies slowly cool down from the orgasmic rush, our gazes collide like an electromagnetic force we can't deny.

Chapter Seven

Lake

IT'S AROUND two in the morning when Cal finally falls asleep. I kiss him one last time before leaving the bed. Carefully, I get dressed and leave through the living room window I left open earlier today. I pull out the phone Derek Farrow gave me and send a text. *Heading to the landing strip.*

Within seconds, my phone rings. I answer immediately as I walk through the back of the trails I was shown when we planned my departure. "Zimmerman here."

"You're *Hawkins*," I hear Dad's voice on the other end.

"I'm both," I remind him. "How are you, Dad?"

"Me?" He groans. "I'm concerned about you. How are you? I heard about your little adventure. You had a knife to your throat, had to flee to a middle-of-nowhere town, and… this isn't what we planned, Lake Sophia Zimmerman Hawkins."

"Wow, did you have to full name me?" I chuckle, knowing he's not just upset but freaking out for his little girl. That's the problem when you're the only girl among many boys. Everyone is too protective of me.

"Cal had some intel about the DiGiacomo Family," I explain. "I was trying to be proactive. How was I supposed to know someone was going to try to kill him?"

He exhales loudly, and before he can say a word, I see the jet that's taking me… well, I don't know where they're taking me because we still need to figure out how to explain my disappearance without raising any suspicion from the FBI.

Once I'm almost there, Dad appears from the shadows. Open arms, big grin, and dark green eyes sparkling. "Hey, sweetheart," he says. I put my phone away before hugging him.

"Hawk, I'm all for family reunions, but we need to go," A voice comes from inside the jet. When I look up, I see Uncle Harrison leaning against the doorframe. "I'm glad you're okay, Lake, but we have to fly to DC. Your mission isn't finished just yet. Ready?"

"Always," I answer, looking back again and hoping Cal finds the message I left him.

My heart hurts because deep down, I don't want to leave him, and in another life, we could've had something. The rest... well, the rest is all a lie.

Chapter Eight

Callahan

WHEN I WAKE UP, Lake is not in bed or the cabin. Did she go back to the hotel? I thought we came to an agreement while we fucked yesterday. Didn't we? She probably went to the small coffee shop she mentioned last night or… I get dressed and head out to look for her.

I'm stopped by Mom. "Good, you live just next door to me. Have they assigned your roommates?" I kiss her cheek and smile.

"You have too much energy. I need coffee," she says.

"Coffee would be nice. Hopefully, Lake is at the coffee shop getting my order."

"I heard Gen is trying to get a job there," she mentions.

I arch an eyebrow. "Where did you hear that?"

"Flora, of course." She glances to our left. "She lives two houses down. Thankfully Leonora isn't here."

"Wife three didn't make it?"

She shakes her head. "No. I wish Suzie…"

Suzie was wife number four. She died of cancer. River and Elle, her children, were just teenagers.

"So the nine of us are here, huh?" I ask, moving along the conversation.

She shakes her head. "No. Slade is…" She waves a hand. "He's like you."

"We're definitely not the same. I'm an FBI agent, and he's a SEAL. I take it he's on a mission."

"That's what Magnus said."

I kiss the top of her head. "I have to catch up with Lake. I'll talk with you later, Mom."

She nods and waves at me but then calls after me. "I'm glad you two are finally together."

When I get to what I believe is the center of the town, I

see Gael. He says, "I don't know if I should be thankful for you saving us or pissed that you dragged us to…"

Gael is like Switzerland of the Thorndales. He gets along with everyone, and everyone loves him. He has an irresistible charm that has people eating from the palm of his hand.

"Someone tried to kill me. My guess is that any of you were the next ones." I shrug. "It's up to you if you want to thank me or blame me for continuing to live your miserable life. I really don't give a fuck."

He snorts. "Leave it to you to sound badass and disengaged. We both know you're the good boy of the Throndales. Well, there's the professor. Bach is a softie too." He squeezes my shoulder. "Thank you for worrying about us, even when you pretend not to give a shit."

"You're welcome?"

"So, what are you doing on this lovely morning? Already missing your ride or die?"

I frown. "What do you mean?"

"Last night, I was enjoying the quiet night when I saw Lake leave your cabin," he says. "She went through the backwoods, but I didn't follow. I'm guessing you two had a different plan for her."

My fists clench. Did Lake fucking leave without telling me?

"You're turning a magenta color. I'm guessing she didn't kiss you good night?" The sarcasm in his voice doesn't go unnoticed. "Well… while you figure out your little mess, I'm heading to the bar. I heard the hot bartender needs help, and I'm ready to pour her drinks and fill her glasses."

I don't bat an eye at his ridiculous comment. My feet march forward toward the headquarters of Crait Quantum Shield.

"Where is she?" I demand, my voice reverberating off the walls as I enter Finnegan's office.

He lifts a lazy gaze to meet mine. "Who?"

"Lake," I growl, my jaw taut. "Apparently, she left last night."

His lips curl into a smirk as he takes hold of his remote and points it to a screen behind me.

When I twist around, there's a grainy video of a woman inching closer toward a jet, her face unidentifiable in the darkness. She wraps her arms around some man before voluntarily boarding the plane. Is Ryder right about her?

"We're investigating her disappearance," he says.

"You need to find her and bring her back," I exclaim, my tone authoritative.

Finnegan drops his head in disagreement with a shake. "That's impossible. She won't come back, but we'll look into who she is and what happened."

"Do you think she's the mole?"

A thin smile creeps onto his lips. "I'm not sure, but she's no longer your issue—she's ours now. Your job is to stay focused on what you agreed to, and keep your family in line." He meets my eyes with a stern glint. "One slip, and you're out. I don't care if you end up in a ditch or at the bottom of the Atlantic Ocean."

My throat tightens as I steel myself against his words. "And all of our assets? Properties? Finances?"

He flicks his wrist nonchalantly in reply. "We explained yesterday that we have the right people to manage everything during the time you're here." His expression darkens as he continues solemnly, "If you end up needing to change your identity permanently, then we'll liquidate them and convert them accordingly at the moment of transaction."

Taking a deep breath, he adds, "For now, you live under the temporary identity we gave you—Callahan Kershaw—and follow my rules."

A beat passes between us in silence before I speak again. "But for how long?"

"I wish I could give you a timeframe. Unfortunately, every case is different."

"And Lake?"

Finnegan releases a heavy sigh. "I wish I had an answer."

My brow furrows, and I press further, "You think she's dirty?"

He cocks an eyebrow and laughs. Then clears his throat and says, "Sorry, old habits die hard. If you're asking if she could be the mole, then the answer is: I'll look into it."

I rake my fingers through my hair as I tell him about my conversation with Ryder. Finnegan nods slowly and says, "He could be right, or he might be trying to divert suspicion from himself. We have to take this slowly and carefully until we figure everything out, okay? You have to be patient."

It's easy for him to say. He's not trapped in a town that's stuck in the past with people he can't stand and betrayed by the woman he loves.

Me… well, as soon as I'm out, heads will roll, even Lake Zimmerman's. She won't get away unscathed. I'll find her and make her pay for her betrayal.

My heart feels like it's being shattered into a million pieces.

She left me.

She betrayed me.

She… she made me fall for her.

The mere thought of never seeing her again feels like a suffocating weight on my chest, an endless ache I can't escape no matter how hard I try. My whole world has been ripped apart, and I'm left alone, lost and broken, trying to pick up the pieces.

I know I won't forget her, but I won't forgive her.

Do you want to more of Heartwood Lake Secret Billionaires?

Come and visit next September when A Place Like You releases.

PREORDER NOW >>>> https://claudiayburgoa. com/wp/a-place-like-you/

FROM USA Today bestselling author Claudia Burgoa comes a heart-gripping, single mom, age gap, secret billionaire romance.

I DON'T HAVE time for flings.

Love is out of the question.

As a single mom and small-town doctor, my plate is more than full.

BUT WHEN DRAKE KERSHAW, an experienced physician with a mysterious past, comes into my life, I can't resist his charm. He's unlike anyone I've ever met before.

DRAKE IS SMART, charming, and has a heart of gold.

But he's also grumpy and hesitant to let anyone close.

Like the rest of his wealthy family, he's full of secrets.

I wouldn't be surprised if he's dangerous.

I SHOULD STAY AWAY, but how can I when he works in my practice?

AND DESPITE HIS GRUMPINESS, Drake is amazing with my son.

He's patient and kind and has a way of making him laugh that always melts my heart.

Watching them together, I can imagine a future–a future that could never happen.

BUT CAN we find a way to overcome our emotional scars and build a future together?

A PLACE Like You is the first book in the Heartwood Lake Secret Billionaire Series—an emotional rollercoaster of a journey that combines the intense drama of Succession and the hilarity of Schitt's Creek. A must-read.

Dear Reader,

Thank you so much for reading STARTS WITH YOU. The prequel of the Heartwood Lake Secret Billionaires.

This is just the beginning of an eight book journey and I hope you're ready for it.

One of my favorite tropes is Fish out of water. I also love secret identity and family found family.

For the past couple of years I've been plotting this series and though I'm still unraveling a few secrets, I'm ready to embark on this new journey. I hope you join me.

As in all the books that are part of Claudia's multiverse, you'll see a lot of familiar faces, but as always, I promise to make each book a standalone romance.

Thank you again for taking a chance on this book.

If you loved this book as much as I did, please drop a review on Bookbub, Goodreads, and your favorite retailer.

Sending all my love,
Claudia xoxo

 Claudia is an award-winning, *USA Today* bestselling author.

She writes alluring, thrilling stories about complicated women and the men who take their breaths away. Her books are the perfect blend of steamy and heartfelt, filled with emotional characters and explosive chemistry. Her writing takes readers to new heights, providing a variety of tears, laughs, and shocking moments that leave fans on the edge of their seats.

She lives in Denver, Colorado with her husband, her youngest two children, and three fluffy dogs.

When Claudia is not writing, you can find her reading, knitting, or just hanging out with her family. At nights, she likes to binge watches shows or movies with her equally geeky husband.

To find more about Claudia:
    website

Be sure to sign up for my newsletter where you'll receive news about upcoming releases, sneak previous, and also FREE books from other bestselling authors.

Also By Claudia Burgoa

Be sure to sign up for my newsletter where you'll receive news about upcoming releases, sneak previous, and also FREE books from other bestselling authors.

Meant For Me

Finally Found You

Where We Belong

Heartwood Lake Secret Billionaires

A Place Like You

Dirty Secret Love

Love Unlike Ours

Through It All

Better than Revenge

Fade into us

An Unlikely Story

Hard to love

Against All Odds Series

Wrong Text, Right Love

Didn't Expect You

Love Like Her

Until Next Time, Love

Something Like Love

Accidentally in Love

Forget About Love

Waiting for Love

Decker Family Novels

Unexpected Everlasting:

Suddenly Broken

Suddenly Us

Somehow Everlasting:

Almost Strangers

Strangers in Love

Perfect Everlasting:

Who We Are

Who We Love

Us After You

Covert Affair Duet:

After The Vows

Love After Us

The Downfall of Us:

The End of Me

When Forever Finds Us

Requiem for Love:

Reminders of Her

The Symphony of Us

Fall for Me

Fight for Me

Perfect for Me

Forever with Me

Mile High Billionaires

Finding My Reason

Something Like Hate

Someday, Somehow

Standalones

Chasing Fireflies

Until I Fall

Christmas in Kentbury

Chaotic Love Duet

Begin with You

Back to You

Co-writing

Holiday with You

Home with You

Here with You

All my books are interconnected standalone, except for the duets, but if you want a reading order, I have it here ↪ Reading Order

Made in the USA
Columbia, SC
27 July 2023

20844894R00045